For Norina, Sophie, and Paul Roy.
Thank you for being the greatest role models.

www.mascotbooks.com

Penny the Pink Nose Poodle

©2017 Dana DiSante. All Rights Reserved. No part of this publication may be reproduced, stored in a retrieval system or transmitted in any form by any means electronic, mechanical, or photocopying, recording or otherwise without the permission of the author.

For more information, please contact:
Mascot Books
560 Herndon Parkway #120
Herndon, VA 20170
info@mascotbooks.com

Library of Congress Control Number: 2017906414

CPSIA Code: PRRB0817A
ISBN-13: ISBN: 978-1-68401-257-2

Printed in the United States

PENNY
THE
PINK NOSE POODLE

Written by Dana DiSante

Illustrated by Ingrid Lefebvre

There once was a poodle named Penny who lived in the New Castle Pound.

The other puppies in the New Castle Pound liked to play catch and tug rope, but Penny never felt she belonged. She was the only dog with a pink nose.

Every day, Penny watched the poodles with black noses leave the pound with their new families. The families were so excited to welcome a puppy to its forever home. Penny thought *I wish there was a family that would hug, kiss, and love me the same as the other puppies.*

o one wants me to be a part of their family, Penny *ecided. It's because of my pink nose.*

As sad as she was every day, Penny still dreamed of being adopted every night.

Penny imagined a big yard full of toys, treats, and most importantly, a loving family who would welcome her to their home.

One day as Penny was walking outside, she heard someone talking near the pound's entrance, so she tilted her head and raised her ear to listen.

Penny placed her little puppy paws on the gate, jumped up and down, and tried to peek at the entrance, but she could not see over the fence.

"My name is Norina," said the new visitor. It was a sweet older woman who sounded so kind it made Penny wonder, *if she is looking for a poodle to take home, maybe she won't even notice my pink nose.*

Norina explained, "In a little while, I will need to be away from my family, so I thought a puppy would help them to smile during the times they're missing me."

As she was talking, Norina spotted out the window a puppy walking in the grass.

Norina stepped outside and giggled softly to herself when she saw the same puppy jumping to see who was walking toward the fence.

She still could not see the puppy's face, so she opened the gate to find a little poodle wagging her tail.

When Norina stopped to stare at Penny, the nervo poodle thought to herself, *Even if this visitor is as kind and sweet as she sounded, she probably will not adopt me because I look so different.*

Just then, Norina picked up Penny and exclaimed, "What an adorable pink nose!"

She kissed Penny on the top of her nose and knew she found the perfect puppy to take home.

As she walked to her car, Norina noticed a glimmer and read the name "PENNY" on the poodle's collar. Norina kissed Penny on the top of her nose again and asked,

"So then, Penny, my 'pink nose poodle,' are you ready to go to your forever home?" Just then, Norina thought she saw the poodle smile.

nny was so happy to finally meet her new
mily. She knew there would always be someone
play with her, take her for walks in the park, and
ss her nose every day.

NEW CASTLE
POUND

Penny's new family surrounded her with love and attention. She knew she was finally where she was meant to be.

Penny's nose didn't make her feel different anymore because she found a family that loved her exactly as she was. Penny found the perfect home.

ABOUT PENNY

Penny was rescued from an animal shelter by Norina, who introduced her to the rest of her family. Penny always fills her family's heart with joy and is a reminder to show love and kindness to others in need.

Have a book idea?
Contact us at:

info@mascotbooks.com | www.mascotbooks.com